CLOUD PAINTINGS

ALSO BY VERONICA BRIGHT

FICTION

A Gift From The Horse Chestnut Tree:
Sometimes Love Hurts
- a second collection of prize winning stories

NON-FICTION

Frogs in Assembly:
Plays for Children in Key Stage One
Published by Kevin Mayhew

Robots in Assembly:
Plays for Children in Key Stage One
Published by Kevin Mayhew

CLOUD PAINTINGS

~ Facing life's challenges ~

A collection of prize-winning stories

Veronica Bright

Published in Great Britain, 2016

All rights reserved.
No part of this publication may be reproduced, stored in a retrieval system, or transmitted in any form or by any means, electronic, mechanical, photocopy, recording or otherwise, without prior written permission of the copyright owners. Nor can it be circulated in any form of binding or cover other than that in which it is published and without similar condition including this condition being imposed on a subsequent purchaser.

ISBN: 978-1534626973

British Cataloguing Publication data:
A catalogue record of this book is available from the British Library

This book is also available as an ebook.

*For Roy
with love and thanks*

CONTENTS

Into The Rain	1
The Gardener	11
Cloud Paintings	20
A Perfect World	38
A Hole in the Sky	51
Shoes	64
The Tightrope Walker	70
Author's comments: Cloud Paintings ~ Facing life's challenges ~	82

INTO THE RAIN

The wind comes hurling across the fen, pulling the grass, jagging at ponds and puddles and dykes. Wires loop from pole to pole, straining. The early morning rain lashes front doors, streaks windows.

There is a face behind one of the panes. A woman in her mid-thirties watches her eldest, a girl, encased in anorak and hood. She crouches beneath a fading rucksack, holds out a wet hand to open the gate, leans into the weather. The girl glances back. The woman smiles, waves, hides the strain.

In the kitchen, Carrie, aged six, feeds her small brother with toast.

'I'll ring the school,' the woman says. 'I'll tell them you're sick.'

Carrie nods, watches her mother, who sighs, starts making sandwiches, slicing tomatoes and cheese.

'Can we have crisps?' Carrie asks.

Her mother closes her eyes.

'I wish you'd say please.'

The girl looks down. 'Please, Mum.'

'OK. Oh, look out.'

The small brother is flapping his arms; squares of jammy toast are flipping through the air, and a cup with a lid hits the floor with a thump. Milk dribbles out, white against the red vinyl.

Then the boy starts rocking backwards and forwards in his high-chair, faster and faster. The woman goes to the sink, rinses a flannel, wipes the sticky, wriggling two-year-old, ignoring his protest. Tears prick her eyes. She unfastens the straps, lifts the boy. He squirms and struggles, refuses his mother's embrace.

She turns back to the picnic, packs the sandwiches into plastic boxes, washes a bunch of grapes.

'I don't like grapes,' says Carrie. Her mother sighs, presses her lips together. Silently she adds a couple of small oranges to the bag.

After an early lunch, it's time to get the children ready for the journey. Carrie wants a ponytail, and for once she keeps still while her mother brushes her hair. Darren runs away as soon as he spots the comb, then stands rubbing his head till his curls are tangled and tousled.

'Keep still, will you?' says his mother, and he throws himself on the floor and cries, thumping his fists.

Finally the children are in their coats and boots. Darren tugs at his buttons, shouting, 'Hot. Hot.'

'It's not hot outside,' says his mother, pulling on her anorak. 'You'll see.'

The woman puts Darren into the car first, leaning forward to fasten his straps, while rain attacks the back of her jeans and soaks her feet. The child then hollers loudly as Carrie is fetched, and fastened into her seat. This is not a good day for the journey.

The front door is locked, the picnic stowed away. The woman starts the engine, glances in the mirror at her daughter's face, at the small pointed features, the pale skin. A miniature version of herself. I used to be pretty like that, she thinks. She sighs, and backs into the road. Darren stops crying, and before long Carrie is singing her usual song.

'We're going to see my dad today,

We're going to see my dad today.

I am very happy cos

We're going to see my dad.'

Fifty-four miles later, they arrive. Carrie is excited, and Darren's asleep. He's not pleased at being woken, at the cold rain streaking his face, the indignity of being carried when he wants to walk.

'Keep up, Carrie, love,' says the woman, and finally, finally, they're through the doors, through security; they're finding a table, taking off dripping coats, and hanging them on the backs of the red plastic chairs. Carrie struggles out of her boots and into the slippers her mother has brought for her. Darren is eager to go and play in the crèche area. He resents having his boots removed. His mother is embarrassed by his frantic yells. Then he's free, and off to play with the nice lady with the badge on. Carrie sits beside her mother, legs swinging neatly.

The woman looks round at the other people, says hello to one or two, avoids catching the eye of the fierce character with the perpetual frown, two tables away. The door at the far end opens; an officer with an Alsatian takes up his place against the wall. It opens again. A man is led in, taken to one of the tables, obliged to sit on the yellow chair assigned to him. Six times the door opens and closes. Six times the woman's heart lurches in her chest. Six times she hopes it will be him. Neil. And then the seventh time it is, it really is. She stands up; she is crying. They are looking at each other. They are allowed a swift hug; they gather Carrie into the embrace. And Darren comes running over to be swung up into his father's arms.

For five, ten minutes, the children are the centre of attention. Then Darren runs off to tell the crèche lady his daddy is here, look that's him, that man there.

Carrie fetches some colouring pens and paper from the corner, comes straight back, stands beside her father as he looks at his wife.

'Anna,' he says.

They talk quietly, the whole world reduced to three red chairs and a yellow one, set round a table. They speak of Scarlet, their eldest child, who goes to the comprehensive, who visits her father in the school holidays. Anna shows Neil a photo of Scarlet on her mobile phone. He strokes the screen gently with one finger.

'I hope she remembers to go to Grandma's after school,' says Carrie.

'She'll remember,' says Anna.

'How is she, your mother?' asks Neil.

'Still upset.'

Angry, if the truth were known.

'But she helps you.'

'I'm her daughter. She helps me.'

Darren comes back to show his father a fire engine he's found in the crèche.

'There'll be trouble later,' says Anna, 'because he won't be allowed to take it home.'

'You coping?'

How can she say she isn't? He'll only lie in his bed worrying about her. She wants him to think of her smiling, happy, like they were on the beach last summer; the girls digging castles, Darren dropping pebbles into a bucket of water.

'I'm fine. Honestly. But I do miss you.'

'That's my girl. My beautiful girl.'

It was the right answer.

Neil gives Carrie some money.

'Take your brother over to the sweet counter,' he says.

'Me, me, me,' calls Darren, and his father laughs.

'Carrie's got the money.'

Darren stares. It's a look Anna knows well.

'Come on Darren,' says Carrie. She skips off. Anna is relieved to see Darren run after his sister.

'Dear of them,' says Neil.

'Mum says she'd like us to go on holiday with them in the summer. Me and the children.' Anna bites her lip. 'A caravan. Norfolk maybe. Near the sea.'

'You're not going, are you?'

'I thought the kids might like it.'

'She'll be on at you again. Brainwashing I call it. You're so sweet, you never notice what she's like.'

'She's my mum, Neil. She only says what she thinks best.'

'Nosey old—'

'No Neil. Don't get upset. I won't go if you don't want me to. It's just that sometimes I could do with a bit of a break.'

'Yeah. I could do with one of those, too.'

Anna holds herself still, determined not to cry.

'Aw,' says Neil. He fidgets, looks away. 'She hates me, you know.'

Anna gives her head the tiniest of shakes.

'Anna.'

She looks anxiously at Neil. 'Are you OK?'

'Fine. You?'

'I'm fine.'

When did she learn to lie to him?

They sit looking at each other. Neil reaches out to touch Anna's hand.

'It'll be over one day,' he says.

She gives a small nod.

'Don't be moody with me,' he says. 'I couldn't stand that. You've come all this way. For God's sake make an effort.'

He looks away, then back.

'I'm reading a book,' he says. 'Yeah, thought that would surprise you.'

He chats on, and Anna relaxes a little. For just a few minutes she is not the careworn mother Scarlet's friends see; not the exhausted parent Carrie's teacher knows; not the woman barely in control of 'that' two-year-old at the mother and toddler group. Nor is she the unfortunate daughter who married the wrong man.

It is time to go. Anna and the children make their way out to the car. Darren wants to kick the water in the puddles. Carrie whines, says she's cold, hungry.

'We'll stop for the picnic soon,' she says.

'I like grapes now,' says Carrie, 'not oranges.'

Inside the prison walls, Neil is taken back to his warm cell. He picks up his book. Just time for a chapter before dinner.

The wind comes hurling across the fen, pulling the grass, jagging at ponds and puddles and dykes. Wires loop from pole to pole, straining. The rain lashes the front doors of houses; streaks all the windows in its path.

THE GARDENER

If I was a bird, I'd be a snipe, a little jack snipe. Keeps his head down, so to speak. In the face of danger, he'll crouch, motionless, rather than fly off. Camouflaged against the reed beds. See a picture of him, and you think he'd be easy to spot — with those perky pale stripes on his head, that speckled buff and white chest, that longish beak. But he fades into the background, disappears.

I put seed on the bird table every day, make sure the water bowl's clean, check the fat balls. Mum used to sit by the window and watch — a pair of blackbirds, a robin, sparrows. Come spring and the blue tits return. They use the nest box every year. I like them all, though Mum said the pigeons were far too greedy, and as for the magpies, they never thought of anyone but themselves.

I miss her. I miss the conversations.

'What did you see today, Roland?' she'd say, and I knew what she meant straight away.

She used to listen while I told her. We get a lot of birds in that big garden. I've worked for the National Trust for years. I love it, gardening. I've got a reputation for working hard, getting on with the job. I ignore the sniggers.

'Sticks and stones, Roland,' Mum used to say. 'Sticks and stones.'

It wasn't true though. Words do hurt.

I've seen head gardeners come and go, heard them described as a breath of fresh air, full of ideas, bursting with enthusiasm. After a few years, off they go to pastures new.

Once I thought I had a chance. Put my name forward. I could do it, I thought. I've got ideas.

I told Mum I'd applied. She hesitated. I know she didn't want me to make a fool of myself. I've got a bit of a stutter, see, besides the other thing.

'Are you sure you're up to this, Roland? It's just that you're, well, let's face it, you're excruciatingly shy. Would you be able to speak up in a meeting, to tell the other gardeners what you want them to do?'

Several days before the interview, I was in front of the mirror, practising my answers. I'd talk about that cottage garden I've always fancied; I'd tell them I'd introduce some different apple trees, old Cornish varieties; specialise in fuchsias.

The interviews were held in the big house. Four of us there were. The other three came the day before, two blokes and a girl. They looked around. The girl waved her arms a lot, very excited she was. One of the men had written a book.

Suddenly it was as clear as anything. I was going to make myself ridiculous.

Come the morning of the interview, I walked round the garden at home, panicking. Should I, shouldn't I? Did I have the courage? I startled a blackbird, and it went over the hedge like an arrow, shrieking out a warning.

I rang from my mobile, said I was sick. Couldn't face looking a complete fool, not in front of those people. I went out and walked all day. Told my mum I didn't get the job. She thought I wouldn't talk about the interview because I was upset.

Silent most of the time. That's your jack snipe. But when he does give voice, it's like a distant cantering horse — ogogok-ogogok-ogogok. Hides away he does. Difficult to locate. Sometimes in the garden, when I'm weeding, hidden away at the back of the wide borders, I hear a whirr of wings, and watch a jay fly away, fast and furious. Or there's a great tit singing 'tea-cher, tea-cher, tea-cher,' or maybe I catch a green woodpecker laughing from a distant tree.

I still go to the marshes on a Sunday. I wear a khaki anorak, trousers the same, and a dull green hat, the one Mum made. I take my binoculars, my telescope, the camera, my lunch. The hide's not very busy in winter. I see a lot of common blackbacks, cormorants, reed buntings. The grey heron's usually around somewhere, hunched up as if he's impersonating an old man in a bus shelter. I open up the shutters and sit on the bench, and sometimes I get lucky. Last weekend I saw some sanderling, and a pair of pochards.

Before Mum was ill, she used to come out to the marshes with me. She preferred the spring, when her hands didn't go numb holding the binoculars, and the wind didn't seep into the hide through every crack. You can see a lot of birds down here in the spring, the usual gulls of course, but other species too. I like it when the terns come, dancing in the air, swooping on delicate wings, snatching at the water's surface, soaring gracefully upwards once more.

That job's come up again. Head gardener. The last chap tried a cottage garden, but somehow he didn't pull it off. In the old days they used to put vegetables in amongst the flowers, didn't they? I'd like to try that. I still hanker after those old apple trees.

Before Mum died, she said, 'I've always tried to be on your side, Roland. I haven't held you back, have I?'

I looked at her. 'No,' I said. 'I don't think so.'

Just after I left school, Mum took me to the Isles of Scilly. She booked for the middle of October, when there would be all kinds of birds in passage. She thought I'd come out of my shell a bit, mixing with like minds, talking to ornithologists day and night. We went by boat — I couldn't face flying; it turned my stomach over just thinking about it. We saw a sooty shearwater from the Scillonian. I was ecstatic. Mum thought the best bit was seeing the islands in the distance, getting closer and closer, the sun glinting on the water, the waves pouring over the rocks.

We stayed in a guest house on St Mary's. Mum said it was wonderful, home cooked food, and no washing up, and weren't the other guests friendly? They wanted to know everything we'd seen, where it was, what time, etcetera. Sometimes I went and sat in my room after dinner, and left Mum in the lounge with the others. I looked up the birds we'd seen, and learnt a bit more about them.

On alternate days we caught a boat out to one of the other islands. The rest of the time we spent on St Mary's. We found all the bird hides, every single one. Went for a walk round the coast one day. Came across a whole crowd of bird-watchers. All lined up along the hedge they were. Several of them had huge telescopes. Bigger than the one I've got now.

'What are you looking at?' Mum asked.

'Hawfinch.'

'They're rare, aren't they? Hear that, Roland? A hawfinch.'

It could have been on the moon for all I could see.

'Here, have a look through this,' one man said, and next minute Mum was oohing, and saying what a beautiful bird it was. I stood there, wondering when we were going to move on. Mum took my arm, led me up to the telescope.

'Go on Roland,' she said. 'Have a look.'

I put my eye to the lens, and there it was, as if it was next to me. It had bluish-black edges to its wings, quite a dark back, a sort of orangey-brown head, a grey collar. Huge, powerful bill. Short tail. I looked him up later. Sixteen and a half to eighteen centimetres long, he was.

Another time we were down by the beach. There was a crowd there, too. Pointing cameras, poor little thing. A girl said it was a snow bunting, blown off course, probably from Scandinavia or Greenland. I thought it was shivering. It looked lost, lonely, and Mum said it wouldn't survive. Cameras clicked, more people arrived, and I didn't know what to do. That poor little bird, all alone in the world. Later, in my room, I wept.

One day we got up before dawn, made our way to a hide by a marshy lake. We were silent, watching, waiting. Then I leaned towards the window, slowly, gently, and looked down into the reeds, and there he was, bobbing up and down, up and down, as if he was on a spring. A jack snipe.

'The finest little fellow I've ever seen,' said Mum. She looked at me and blinked back a tear.

I used to rely on Mum a lot, let her do the talking, make the decisions. Now it's up to me. Four cups of tea went cold before I picked up a pen, applied for the job. I found myself talking to her.

'This could be my last chance, Mum. The cottage garden, the fuchsia border, the Cornish apple trees. The whole place would be like my very own garden.'

And now I'm here, waiting. The door of the interview room opens, and they call my name. I unclench my fists. Not fleeing in the face of danger. Not this time.

I want to make my mum proud of me. Even though she's dead. So I'm standing my ground, in spite of the stutter, and my face not being quite what it should be.

I walk into the room, pretending to be bold against the fear.

Like I said, if I was a bird, I'd be a little jack snipe.

CLOUD PAINTINGS

It's a shock, seeing him again. I turn away, peer at one of the pictures; try to concentrate on the two figures on a boat, bent over in labour, oblivious to the blue of the sky, the lightly moving waves.

I have to glance back. It is him, isn't it? He's with a much younger woman. Her hair falls over one shoulder. Her floral dress speaks of the day outside, of country gardens, roses. I have to know who she is.

They've stopped in front of some oil paintings — huge dark clouds, churning, full of rain. They speak to each other. He's wearing a zip-up jacket, beige or cream, it's difficult to tell from here. He's holding a cap, the sort that always makes me think of him on that little sailing boat.

Are they a couple? They're certainly lost in their conversation.

'Come on, Anna.'

I follow my companions towards the counter with its wine glasses in neat lines. They could be an exhibit. A man comes in, puts a tray of tartlets down. We sit on bar stools and discuss the work. I don't know anything about technique; I can simply say which pictures I like, whereas Polly and Clay can dissect the style and refer to other artists who paint in a similar way. I'm sure they've only brought me here because they think I should get out more.

He looks up once. I almost catch his eye. I turn hastily, pick up one of the dainty nibbles, concentrate on eating it. Polly is waving her hands, talking about the 'kinetic energies of the sea' in somebody's 'mixed media' work.

'So dramatic,' says Clay, seriously.

To be honest I find some of this stuff unfathomable.

I can't keep my eyes away from him. It's been a long time, and still I feel the same ache, the same heartbreaking longing.

The couple move on, sit on one of the leather sofas. He leans back, studying the artwork on the wall ahead of him. She's more on the edge of her seat, half turned towards him. The summery dress is riding up over her knees. I can see her shiny red shoes, at least four inches of heel. She's younger than me, by a number of years.

I reach for a tartlet, force my attention onto the sharpness of the cheese. I'm thinking about his younger son, and all he went through. Sam. I can see him now, straight brown hair, those trusting eyes. When he came into school each day, his mother was never far behind. She used to make sure he hung up his coat, put his book bag and packed lunch in the right places. For most of the four-year-olds in my class these were simple jobs, but for Sam they were too taxing. His mother encouraged him, always, but I knew how much she worried.

What happened to her was completely unexpected. The first I knew of it was when little Charlie's mum appeared at the classroom door with Sam one morning. He blinked as he looked from one of us to the other.

'I'll put your book bag in the box, Sam,' she said. 'Run along now, go and play with Charlie.'

Sam hesitated.

'I'll tell your teacher,' she said.

It was like being hit in the stomach, news like that. Lauren Scott had suffered a terrible asthma attack.

She was dead.

I'd seen her the day before. She'd been in the classroom, laughing with Sam. She'd teased him, and hugged him as if she couldn't bear to give him up to me for the day. The only day she had left. Her last day.

'They've not told Sam yet,' Charlie's mum whispered, and I knew we were both wondering how he was going to cope, because he'd shared everything with Lauren — the difficulty of learning to read, the pain of a scraped knee, a bruised shin, all the triumphs of playtime goals.

When Charlie's mother left, there was Sam waiting outside the classroom. He looked at me solemnly.

'My mum's in hospital,' he said.

I fought back tears. 'Charlie's mum told me.'

When the rest of the children came in, Sam stood and watched them, the chatterers, the timid, the self-reliant, the ones who needed constant encouragement and praise. Then he crossed the room slowly, and went to sit in his place beside Charlie. I asked everyone to be quiet, please, and I called the register on the first day of Sam's new life.

*

Richard Scott. Sam's father. I remember him standing at the school gate that afternoon, eyes on the ground. The poor man looked worn out, his mind somewhere else.

'Is Mummy home yet?'

That was the first thing Sam said, desperate for the reply. His dad shook his head.

'I want a word with your teacher. Go and talk to Charlie and his mum.'

I looked across the playground. Charlie's mother wasn't smiling. She gathered Sam into her arms, and hugged him.

'Come on.' Charlie was eager to have the freedom of the playground for five minutes, to chase his football, his skinny legs racing, one shoe-lace untied and flicking. Sam hesitated for only a second. Football with Charlie was what he came to school for. Off he went, and for the next few minutes he forgot his mother, and the fact that she wouldn't be at home making his tea, giving him a bath, reading him a story.

'We haven't told him yet.' Richard Scott wiped the back of his hand across one eye. 'We've said she's in hospital.'

I couldn't speak. He'd always been so strong, so confident. Now he seemed diminished, fragile.

'Has he been OK?' he asked.

I shook my head almost imperceptibly. I looked across the playground as Sam and Charlie chased the ball, legs flying along, arms helping them to balance as they swerved and kicked.

'He's been quiet.'

'We think it's best if he comes to school as usual.'

I nodded.

'I'm so sorry,' I said.

Richard looked down, pinched his nose.

'There'll be an inquest.'

He crossed the playground, and Sam ran over to hold his hand. Charlie carried on kicking and racing.

And Sam went home to wait for news that would never come.

*

Richard Scott. After all these years. Sam must be seventeen by now, a young man, tall like his father I expect. I wonder if he is still a scatterbrain, whether his friendship with Charlie has stood the test of time. I picture them watching football on a Saturday afternoon, green and white scarves at their throats, singing along with the crowd, yelling at the ref.

But what of Richard? He looks as if he has survived better than I have. He's talking animatedly with his companion. Both of them keep looking up at the cloud paintings. I study these again, from my stool by the bar. Their sense of brooding is almost unbearable. They speak to me of time misspent, of a love that was never returned.

Richard used to own a small Mirror dingy; he took his boys out in the bay at weekends. I watched them sometimes, as I walked up and over the hill, on my way home from the bakery. The elder boy, Jack, was a natural sailor. Father and son were a pleasure to watch together, a team. Sam didn't have the same ability. I saw the beam clomp him on the head more than once. Sometimes the little boat would sway dangerously, and Richard's voice would carry across the water as he issued reprimands and instructions.

'He'd rather be in the park with a ball,' Sam's mother told me. 'He takes after me. I'm a landlubber. But that's all right. We understand each other, Sam and I.'

My companions have finished their drinks.

'Another look at Chelsea Danes, I think,' says Polly. 'In the corner.'

Clay leads the way. Polly glances at me.

'You're quiet. Are you OK?'

'I've seen someone I used to know.'

'Want to go and say hi?'

'Maybe. In a minute.'

'Who is it?'

'A parent from the village I used to teach in.'

'I don't know why you ever left.'

I was always telling Polly how wonderful it was. Summer sun, sand between my toes, children running up to show me a shell they'd found, or a long strand of seaweed they had tucked in the back of their trunks like a tail. And in the evening, the view across the bay, the ever-changing colour of the water, the slap of wet-shoes on the slipway, the chatter outside the pub.

We stand in front of a row of watercolours.

'Maybe that one,' says Polly. 'For above the fireplace.'

It's a harbour scene, the water dappled with luminous shades.

'Mm, possible. Can we look at my trees again?' Clay nods towards two larger works. 'I like the effect the acrylics give the sky.'

'I'll just...' I say, and Polly takes up my story. 'Anna's seen someone she knew years ago. Wants to say hello.'

I smile, hiding something I am afraid of. Rejection. I step purposefully towards the brown settee, but falter when I see Richard's companion stand up, hear her speak.

'Won't be long.'

It would have been so much easier to approach him with someone else there. I watch as he studies the grey of the clouds.

'Hello. It's Richard, isn't it?'

He looks up, pushes himself to his feet.

'Anna.'

He shakes my hand.

We sit on the sofa. I am overwhelmed by a sense of the past. It comes gusting at me, a wild wind through tiny streets, waves rollicking over the sea wall, sandbags along the doorsteps. A thick fog muffling the lonely call of a ship's horn, a Cornish dampness creeping through my clothes to reach my skin. The past lives in front of me in those cloud paintings.

'Beautiful, aren't they?' he whispers.

Richard has the palest eyes. He asks me what I'm doing nowadays, and I tell him about the dockside school with its streetwise five-year-olds and the blocks of identical flats.

'Do you still sail?' I ask.

'Do seagulls like fish and chips?'

We laugh.

In the week after Lauren died, he used to come into school at the end of the day. Charlie's mum would ask Sam if he'd like to come and play, have tea with them. Mostly he said yes, because it meant football in the park, and an escape from the depressing atmosphere at home, which he didn't understand.

Every single day he asked his dad the same question.

'Has Mum come back today?'

In the end his father closed his lips, gave a barely perceptible shake of the head. He would watch as Sam and Charlie set off down the hill, lost in a friendship which was echoed in long waving grasses, and the valerian gently swaying from cracks in the old stone walls. Then he would follow me into the classroom, and he would talk.

One day he and Lauren had taken the children to Looe. They ate fish and chips, sitting on the wall beside the river, their legs dangling. Sam had thought seagulls were magnificent till then. They could glide in the air with little effort, or simply fly away when they felt like it. When they strutted up and down beside the harbour, they looked like proud kings. He happened to look round at one which was doing a tight little dance behind him, and wham, a fierce beak was in his chip box and the bird was away with half his battered haddock.

'How are Sam and Jack?' I ask.

Richard talks about Jack. The words flow towards me — Plymouth University, marine biology, scuba diving, loves sailing, enters races, doing very well. Richard talks of his elder son with pride. I smile, but it's Sam I want to know about, sad lost little Sam, a boy who had to survive without the person who understood him better than anyone else.

'Sam? He's almost eighteen now. Didn't know what he wanted to do. Well, he did, but it involved a lot of surfing, beach football, general bumming about.

He's a good swimmer. Did I ever tell you…? Yes, I can see I did.'

It was on one of those after school occasions, when time held its breath, and I hoped, I felt, a beautiful relationship was beginning to grow. Richard told me about a holiday they took, in the little village called Mousehole.

'The day Sam almost drowned.' He shakes his head, retells the story. 'Slipped off the edge of the harbour wall. We thought he'd be alright. We knew he could swim, even though he was only four. You know what kids are like in the wind. High as kites they were; me yelling at them to keep away from the edge. The last thing Sam saw as he went over the side was his mother with both hands over her mouth. Course we rushed straight to the edge, expected to see him bobbing about in the water. There was no sign of him.'

'You jumped in and rescued him.'

'Only after Lauren spotted him, a dark blue shadow right underneath the water. Screaming she was. He went under three times, you know. We both thought we'd lost him.'

Richard looks at his hands, the hands that saved Sam. 'Yeah, nearly eighteen he is now. I think he still misses his mother. I thought he'd get over it quickly, being so young. I've tried to be a mother and father to him.'

I nod.

'Did you ever find a partner?' he asks.

I shake my head.

'You were a good listener. Stopped me going mad, those talks we had.'

'I let you down.'

Richard looks at me, realises I'm crying.

It was the second week after Lauren died. Sam was still asking the same question at home time every day. I could tell he endured school, but only because it would bring him closer to the time he believed his mother would come back. His mind limped through the demands I made of it, from the weighing table to the counting activities, the literacy session, small voices repeating phonic sounds, recognising letter combinations, reading words. At home his father was striving to remain cheerful. Jack knew, but was sworn to secrecy. On the day of the funeral, Jack was missing from school, but Sam was there as usual.

The children were in a group on the carpet. I told them a story, about a boy who wanted to be better at scoring goals than anybody else in his class. Even the girls were caught up in the idea of being the best. Each child's eyes were upon me, believing it could be so. There was a pause when I finished, one of those beautiful mini-silences where the children are lost in private moments of confidence in their own ability.

'I'm going to tell my mum that story when she comes home,' said Sam.

'Sam, she's not coming home.'

Somebody had to say it, somebody had to tell him.

He looked at me, trusting every word I said.

'Your mum's dead.'

I think each child in that room imagined their own mother, pegging out washing, baking a cake, tucking them up in bed at night.

Sam didn't cry. He nodded a few times. He already knew it was true.

Charlie's mum came to school to fetch Sam that day. His father and Jack were still busy at the village hall, where friends and relations had crowded after the funeral. Everyone except Sam.

Richard never came into school for a chat again. I knew I had blown it, a friendship that might have turned into something else; that I hoped desperately would turn into something else.

He was too busy to come to school on sports' day. He avoided parents' evening at the end of term, by which time I had handed in my notice. He didn't come to my leaving party, and it was only me who knew how much that mattered.

I still miss the village, the close community life, the Spar shop and the post office. But most of all I miss Richard.

I stare at the deep grey cloud pictures, and I know this is the moment I've dreaded for thirteen years.

'I was the one who told Sam his mother was dead.'

Richard looks at me.

'I know.' The next moment is silent, and seems like an hour.

'I couldn't do it,' he says. 'A trusting little face he had. I thought that if I told him, he'd have felt I was the one who'd killed her.'

He shifts in his seat, and he has that same vulnerable look that Sam had.

'I was a coward,' he says. 'You did the right thing.'

Richard's companion comes towards us. We both get up.

'My niece. Jenny's an art buff. Thought I needed a bit of education.'

'We'd better go,' says the niece, then adds pointedly, 'Your wife will be waiting for us. She's expecting a baby. Their first.'

'My third,' says Richard. He grins. 'So good to have bumped into you.'

'Remember me to Sam and Jack.'

'I will.'

I'm reluctant to leave the moment, but the niece is pulling Richard's sleeve.

He smiles, and as I watch them leave, I hear her voice, a little too loud. 'I thought you looked as if you needed rescuing.'

'Not at all.' I can just hear his reply. 'That lady once rescued me.'

I re-join Polly and Clay, who have decided not to buy after all.

'Ready to go?' they ask.

'Almost.' I struggle to hide the deep sadness that is threatening to drown me. 'I'd like just one more look.' I can hardly finish the sentence.

'What at?'

I turn away from them so they won't see my face.

'Those… wonderful… cloud paintings.'

A PERFECT WORLD

Nought to sixty in 5.5 seconds.

Thomas loves the feeling, cruising in the third lane, checking the mirror for the 'nee-naws', as his daughter calls them. Everything's hunky-dory, and he's alone in a perfect world.

Hunky-dory. That was always one of his mother's favourite words. He passes a lorry, and sighs. He remembers why this journey north is so difficult.

He hasn't been there for... how long? Guilt rides in the car with him. Harriet is nearly three, and he's never taken her there. His mother's been up to London of course. The house is small so she has to stay in a hotel. Meg said they could make room, but he wouldn't hear of it.

Thomas pulls into a service station for a coffee. The menu advertises those pancakes Harriet loves so much. Thomas wishes he had more time for his family. He often has to bring work home. The pay's good though, and he is able to buy Harriet all kinds of treats, cherry pancakes with ice cream being one of them. He really should make more time for family outings.

And yet... He's never really happy unless he's alone, is he? There are times when he longs to be all those things he imagines the perfect parent to be: patient, interested, kind. He knows he is generous. His own parents gave him expensive presents, didn't they? He sips his coffee, and remembers the bike they bought him for his fifth birthday. It was superb, the envy of the neighbourhood children. But he'd done something so bad, his parents had put the bike into the loft for three months, and when it came out again, it didn't seem so wonderful after all.

'Has it shrunk?' he wanted to know.

'It's an illusion.'

He frowned, puzzling over this new grown up word.

'You've got somewhat taller during the school holidays, that's all,' his mother said.

He has a sudden urge to go back to that first house. He had a climbing frame in the garden. Once, at the park, he'd pushed that prissy dark-haired girl off a swing. He'd wanted a go himself, and that seemed the best way to solve his problem at the time. Now he remembers his mother's exasperation. Why wouldn't he share? Take turns?

'I don't understand you,' she said.

In Thomas's mind he can see their former house clearly, set in a quiet cul-de-sac. That bike was something else. He used to take it outside and the crowd would gather, small eyes looking at it longingly, little fingers stroking it, somebody squeezing the hooter. He used to laugh, push their hands away, and ride off along the pavement shouting, 'Can't catch me!' No way would he let that lot have a go on *his* bike.

Thomas drains the last of his coffee, sets down the cup, resumes his journey.

Nought to sixty in 5.5 seconds. Again he experiences the satisfaction of speed, of driving away from problems, cruising fast and free. His mobile rings and he ignores it. He's made up his mind.

He detours to go and park outside the house where his childhood began. He gets out of the car, and presses the key fob switch. The locking system gives a satisfying clunk.

The front door is the same, polished oak. He rings the bell. He hears someone coming, prepares a charming smile.

'I'm sorry to bother you. I used to live here,' he says.

The woman turns her head slightly, peers at him.

'My name's Thomas Dawson. Does that mean anything to you?'

'Well!' The woman breaks into a smile. 'We bought the house from the Dawsons... Must be thirty years ago.'

She calls her husband who emerges to say hello. They invite him in.

Thomas steps over the doorstep, into the past. Immediately he feels frustrated, oppressed. He fights a desire to escape. He follows the couple into the lounge, looks around.

'It's very different,' he says.

'I know,' says the woman. 'We've brought up three children here, so our furniture had to be pretty sturdy.' She smiles. 'Your parents had some beautiful things.' Then she sighs, and shakes her head. 'Those cabinets full of exquisite pieces!'

'Wedgwood, Royal Doulton, etcetera,' says Thomas. He can almost see them again, cold behind the glass.

'And that gorgeous pale carpet! We inherited it, but I'm afraid we had to replace it after a few years. The children, you know. And their friends.'

'I was never allowed to play in here,' says Thomas. The old resentment eats into him.

The man makes Thomas a cup of tea while the woman continues to talk, leading the way into the dining room. The polished table has gone, of course. Suddenly he remembers why they took his bike away from him. He'd been banging on that magnificent table with his fork. He'd screamed at them in frustration, thumping his fork down, on and on, bang, bang, bang, leaving rows of tiny holes in the virgin wood. He wouldn't stop till they forced him out of the room, banished him from their sight.

Then he has a flashback to last week, when he'd hollered at Harriet for a similar misdemeanour.

'I don't know how your parents managed to keep such a beautiful home with a youngster and his friends tearing around,' says the woman.

'I wasn't allowed to have children in,' says Thomas, and his mother's words echo in his ears. 'No-one wants to play with a naughty boy like you.'

He clenches his fists, and then straightens his hands again, a habitual gesture as he tries to remain calm. He feels uncomfortable. He wants to leave, to speed away.

The woman is pointing out at the garden, where Thomas had his climbing frame. Now there's a toddler's swing.

'For my granddaughter.' She picks up a photograph. 'There's nothing like the blessing of grandchildren. Mind you, sometimes you need the patience of a saint.'

Again Thomas thinks of his mother and Harriet.

'Believe me,' says the man, coming in with the tray, 'children are another species.'

Back in the car, Thomas forces himself to concentrate. Only half an hour and he'll be there. It's not so easy to sit in a cosy nought to sixty bubble on these country roads. Besides, new thoughts crowd his head with every bend. The memory of his mother persists. There she is, neat and tidy, polishing the brasses, wiping sticky fingerprints off the walls. Why oh why had she always wanted everything to be so clean and sparkling? So perfect. She'd have been better off with a nice quiet girl, he thinks; a girl to match the pale pink carpet, bows in her hair, and pretty manners. Instead of which she had a boy, certainly not a docile, do-as-you're-told one.

He slows to take a double bend. The light in the sky is changing. Surely there was nothing wrong with asking questions? He wasn't worse than any of the other boys who lived in the cul-de-sac, was he? His mother, his bossy, fussing mother, had no idea what children were really like. The words of the man back at the house return to him. Children are a different species.

How many times has he been frustrated with Harriet? Too exhausted and irritable to listen to Meg? He sees that perhaps he is just like his father was, always busy, a responsible job making too many demands, taking its toll. Thomas admits he leans heavily upon Meg for solace. Kind, calm Meg.

When did he last make Meg a cup of tea?

Perhaps the expensive gifts Thomas received as a child were an apology for the time his father spent away from him. Perhaps his mother resented having a small child she hadn't asked for. Now Thomas finds life so hectic, he has barely any time for Harriet. No wonder Meg wants them to give it all up and move to the country.

'That's impossible Meg,' he'd said. 'What would I do in the country?'

'People find jobs in the country as well as here,' she'd replied. 'Or they commute. A train journey can be quite relaxing, you know.'

She'd said she'd like to see Harriet running across the fields, finding wild flowers, feeding ducks.

'We have ducks in London, Meg,' he'd said, 'in the park.'

'I'd like another baby, Tom.' Then she'd gone on quickly. 'And I want to grow vegetables, maybe keep chickens.'

'Chickens, Meg. Are you out of your mind?'

He pulls into his mother's drive.

The live-in carer opens the door, and leads the way into the drawing room. The same antique cabinets are full of the same beautiful things. Thomas's mother reclines on a chaise longue, a blanket over her knees.

'Hello Mother.'

'You came alone then?'

'Meg couldn't get the time off...' His voice tails away. He feels five years old again, a naughty boy.

'I'll make some tea,' says the carer.

'Do sit down, Thomas. You're making the place untidy.'

'I always did that Mother,' says Thomas, almost savagely. Then he stops. 'I'm sorry. It's been a long journey.'

His mother is silent. She looks tired. Thomas takes his case upstairs. Do we all end up stuck in some dreadful caricature of ourselves, he wonders, unable to break free?

He goes downstairs to where his mother waits. Her hair is beautifully styled; her make-up is tasteful. Thomas sees the effort she has made for his visit. Yet the illness is winning. She looks terrible.

The carer brings in a tray. She gives no hint of disapproval that he hasn't visited for months.

Thomas attempts to speak calmly of Harriet, and Meg. From the distant kitchen come the sounds of a meal being prepared, a song on the radio.

A silence falls between them. Shadows gather in the room.

'I went back to our first house today, Mother,' he says.

He tells her about the people who moved in after they'd left, the people who stayed for thirty years.

'You hid my bike from me. Do you remember that?'

Thomas watches as his mother shuts her eyes.

'I found you such a difficult child, Thomas,' she says. He strains his ears to hear her. 'I didn't understand you.'

He thinks of Harriet. He doesn't understand her, not at all. She's so… alive, yes, that's the word, alive.

'I do love you, Thomas.'

The words spill into the gloom of the impeccable room, as if his mother has to say it while there is still time.

'I wanted to be the perfect parent,' she says.

A log shifts in the fire. The clock ticks. From the kitchen the six o'clock pips announce the news

'I wish…'

'What do you wish, Mother?'

'That I could have another go at it all. But as they say, life isn't a rehearsal.'

Thomas needs to do something, anything, to prevent the anguish and guilt and the desire to weep.

'I'll pull the curtains, shall I?'

He stands beside the window, looks out at the darkening sky. The first star gives a gentle welcome to the night.

'Mother.' He tries hard to see things from her point of view. He walks over to her, and takes her hand.

'Growing up in the country was good,' he says. 'I don't really care about the bike, you know.'

'I'm so tired,' is all she replies.

Later, in the bedroom that overlooks the hills, Thomas has time to think. He has a future, God willing. It's time be the person he wants to be. He imagines Harriet playing in a sunny garden; Meg picking flowers, growing vegetables, her weary frown long gone. Maybe feeding chickens. Maybe another child on the way.

Perfect?

No. Alive. He will be alive, like Harriet. And Meg.

Everything will be all right.

Soon it will be tomorrow, and he'll head for London. He may well be singing. Yes. Probably one of Harriet's funny little songs.

Nought to sixty in 5.5 seconds. Not escaping, but going home.

A HOLE IN THE SKY

'You sure you'll be all right, son?'

I press my teeth together, turn my head away. 'I'll be fine.'

'It's just that... well, I could see you to the bus stop, get you on OK.'

I grip the arms of the wheelchair. 'Why don't you come all the way with me? Right into the interview room. Make sure I can manage in the toilet.'

'Douglas.'

I look up. She's got tears in her eyes. I'm twenty-eight years old and I make my mother cry on a daily basis.

'I'll be all right. Got to be, haven't I?'

Mum opens the front door, pale-faced, frowning. 'Just ring me if... if you need me.'

She walks down the path, opens the gate. 'Good luck.'

'Thanks.'

I turn into the street, concentrating. The pavement's not that smooth. I want this job more than I've wanted anything in my whole life. Except one thing perhaps. One person. But I can't have my legs back, can I?

I turn the corner, reach the dip in the kerb. It's difficult to look left and right from down here, with all these parked cars. I was here one day and some well-meaning geezer asked if I wanted to cross; thrust me into the road, in the path of a kid on a bike. Frightened all three of us.

I need a label round my neck. 'Go away. Leave me alone.'

I ease myself off the pavement, hands turning the wheels that manoeuvre me along. Didn't want one of those motorised efforts. Independent. Always have been.

'You trying to prove something?' Mum asked.

'What if I am?'

At the main road, I manipulate myself towards the crossing. The green man flicks to red before I get there. I glance at my watch. Where did all that time go? Mum, yacking at me, she's to blame. I stare towards the bend, and as I wait, the 81 cruises round the corner. It speeds past the bus stop before I can get there, and I swear out loud.

A memory leaps into my head. Nicola, in a dress in that exquisite colour of apple blossom before it starts to fade. She's walking along beside me, in those tall high heels she loved, her hand in mine. Then I had to run for the bus, plead with the driver to wait, just a second, I said, and once he'd seen her, he didn't mind at all.

I mustn't panic. I need a plan. I won't get that job if I'm late.

I wheel myself towards the place where the chain ferry lands. It can't be that hard, getting on in a chair, can it? I know there's a downward slope to manoeuvre, but I've got a brake. The buses are more frequent the other side of the river.

It's got to be done.

It's cold down here by the water. Waves bounce; splashes curl, white-tipped. I wait by the railings and watch as the chain drags and pulls, fighting the tide. The ferry lowers its jaw; it's time to move.

'Want a bit of help, mate?'

'Nah, thanks. I'll be OK.'

I fight the slant of the gradient all the way to the passenger ramp. I stare ahead, brow set. I will do this on my own. My arms ache. My jaw's set. A new challenge every day. Isn't that what I used to love about life?

It's become a mantra I repeat against the uselessness I feel.

I park up in the passenger area, lean back, arms drooping. I catch a woman staring at me. She looks away quickly, but I sense something, in that glance. Go away, I want to scream, I don't need your pity.

In the distance, beyond the bobbing water, there's a view of the next town. White houses, slate roofs. The bridge. The road where it happened. I relive the sound of the bike roaring in my ears, the tarmac coming to meet me, the exhilaration of spring and sunshine and speed. Lambs in the fields, catkins in the hedges. Nicola waiting for me at her mum's house. I can't remember the rest. Death was cheated, but the price was freedom.

Departure time. The ferry clanks. I close my eyes, experience the noise, the vibrations. When I was a boy I imagined giant metal legs reaching down to the bottom of the river, sprinting underneath us, thump, thump, thump. All I hear now is desperation.

As we dock the other side, I brace myself. The gradient is not going to defeat me. I start turning my wheels. Immediately one of the ferrymen is behind me, pushing my wheelchair. He's puffing when we reach the road. I force myself to thank him.

'No problem.' He swaggers off, and I catch sight of one of his mates doing an impersonation of him struggling up the slope. Years ago I'd have laughed. These days I don't find anything funny.

A bus arrives at the stop. The driver lowers the platform, and I roll myself on. There's a pushchair opposite my space.

'What's that man doing?' says small voice. 'Why man pushchair?'

I look across at the mother. She's not much more than a girl.

'Hush,' she says.

I stare out of the window, refusing to speak. Why should I help her over her embarrassment, when I'm stuck in this chair, stuck in this life?

When they get off the bus, the child gives me a smile, and a wave. I've left it too late to make it all right.

In the city, the driver lowers the platform, and I get off the bus. And suddenly there's Nicola.

'Um, hi.'

I can't reply. I've only seen her one since I came out of hospital. I put that down to her mother. She wouldn't want her darling daughter saddled with a cripple.

'How are you, Doug?'

All I can do is shake my head.

'Got time for a coffee?'

I look away. 'Going to an interview.'

'Good.'

'Newspaper Offices.'

'I'll meet you afterwards if you like.'

I want to slam off in disgust, push myself away from the girl who abandoned me.

'Why aren't you at work today?' I ask.

She reaches out a hand, ready to ruffle my hair; thinks better of it. 'School holidays,' she says. 'Teachers' playtime.'

I start moving. 'Of course.'

She walks beside me, chatting about the children in her class. Avoiding all mention of the accident, what I've been through. Well, that's what I want, isn't it? I don't want to be somebody people have to pity.

'Will you hear straight away, about your job?'

'I don't know.'

'Meet me for coffee or something? Tell me all about it?'

I pause. That's what I want, isn't it?

Then she drops the bombshell. 'I'm OK for time. I'm not meeting my boyfriend till six.'

It's like being socked in the jaw.

'Ring me when you've finished.' Nicola's finding a pen in her bag, a scrap of paper. 'Here's my number. Good luck, Doug. Heaven knows you deserve it.'

At the newspaper offices, I wheel up to the desk, introduce myself, produce a smile. I want this so much.

I am shown where to wait. A phone rings, someone laughs. A door opens and closes. There are people here with a future, things to look forward to, weekends in the country, holidays in the sun. A girl like Nicola with her hair and her legs. And her smile.

My hands feel hot and clammy. A thin man with sandy hair leads the way into the interview room. There are five people, three men and two women. Sandy-hair introduces them. I force myself not to look down. But I know, I know already. They don't want me, not even the one with the red dress and the kind face. She feels sorry for me, but you don't get offered a job because of that, do you?

I answer their questions. I'm angry with myself at the trite things I come out with. Yes, I can write copy. They have the presentation I submitted in front of them, for goodness sake. Yes, I am willing to start at the bottom and work my way up. What else can I do? I have no choice. People like me have to prove themselves, time and again. And yes, of course I can work under pressure.

That a lie. I can't do anything under pressure any more. I can barely cross the road and catch a bus. My mother is on perpetual alert for me.

'Thank you for coming.' The sandy-haired man looks at me, his face unemotional. 'We'll be in contact after we've made our decision.'

'It was a pleasure to meet you,' says the woman in red. Does she say that to everyone?

I can hardly face the people out in the street. I have nothing. I am a bloke, twenty-eight years old; a cripple who lives with his mother. A caged man. I want to kick something but I can't move my legs. I'm no longer free.

That's not all, is it? I've trapped my mum in the cage with me. Worrying like a dog over a wounded leg, she hovers round me, afraid to let me out, fearful of my state of mind, my temper.

I don't phone Nicola.

I push myself to the bus stop, start the long trek home. A group of youths overtakes me, laughing, teasing each other. My phone beeps. There's a message on the screen.

'Where R U?'

I don't reply. There's no point.

As the ferry clanks its way back across the river, I sit in the bus and watch a seagull ride the wind. That's what freedom is, moving with agility, going where you like.

The bus driver lowers the platform and I get off the bus. I wheel myself along, the gale buffeting my hair. I arrive home exhausted and cold.

'Tell me all about it,' says Mum. She hides behind the usual grey smile.

I shake my head.

'Maybe after tea,' she says. I've disappointed her. Again.

*

I've caught a cold. Mum fusses. She says she knew it would all be too much for me. She's shocked that I went on the ferry as a foot passenger. She says it doesn't matter what those people at the newspaper office think of me. Something else will turn up.

The doorbell chimes and it's Nicola. Mum shows her in.

'You didn't ring.'

'I'll get you a cup of tea, dear.' Mum always had a soft spot for Nicola, thought of her as a future daughter-in-law, probably romanticised about grandchildren, too.

Nicola sits down, puts her bag on the carpet.

'I suppose the interview was bad,' she says after a while. 'That was why you didn't phone.' She looks round the room. 'Not much has changed. Except your mum. She used to be so full of life. When I think of her, she's laughing.'

'She hasn't got much to laugh about these days.'

'You used to be able to make her laugh, Doug. You could always cheer her up. It must be hard for her, seeing someone she loves suffering so much.'

'If you've come here to feel sorry for me —'

'I haven't. I wanted to ask you if you'd like to come to the pub with us, with me and my boyfriend, and a couple of other people.'

'There, I knew you felt sorry for me.'

'You were brave, Doug. But then you were angry, and... I couldn't bear seeing you like it. You were someone I didn't know any more.'

From the kitchen comes the sound of a radio.

'When I met you in town, the other day, I could tell, you were still that angry person. I feel sorry for your mother, because she has to live with you all the time.'

Nicola talks about her job, her boyfriend, her life after me. The world goes on, doesn't it? Life goes on. And Nicola's gone on.

But when I listen to her, she's still the same — young and enthusiastic and wonderful. She's telling me about a kid at school, how he'd brought something for her.

'He was feeling in his trouser pockets, and I ask him what it is. "It's a slug, Miss," he says. You can imagine my face. "A slug?" He carries on fishing about. Then he looks me in the eye. "Bother," he says, "I left in in my other pair."'

Nicola's face is alight with joy, and I laugh, a huge explosion of sound that brings my mother running from the kitchen.

And there's a hole in the sky of my anger.

And I'm telling them about the day I went for the interview, how rolling down the slope onto the ferry was like being on a self-propelled roller-coaster.

'You want to borrow this thing and try it,' I say to Mum, and she fills the room with laughter. Just like she used to.

'The pub, Doug. You will come, won't you?'

I feel happy, like I used to. I nod.

'Thanks,' I say quietly, and my mother's face holds a smile from the past.

SHOES

Sneakers, flip-flops, slip-ons, sandals, stilettos, wedges, lace-ups, brogues.

Shoes. I've seen them all. Trainers, I can name every single make. I can list the popular ones. Built for sport, but never mind that. They've become a kind of universal footwear. Like socks. A lot of people amble along in trainers, which makes a bit of a mockery of them, I'd say. I've seen trainers with the laces removed. Laziness or fashion? Who am I to comment?

Crocs. The kids love them. Boys go for black, navy, blue. Girls choose pink, or purple. Occasionally the ones imprinted with tiny flowers. I like Crocs. They make me think of the beach my mum took me to when we lived down west. I had bare feet, but Crocs would have been good; they help you walk over shells and sharp gritty sand; you could speed over pebbles; jump off rocks.

Last week a pair of slippers walked by. Trodden down at the back; used to be pink I guess. The fur was mangy. Looked like a dog had played with them for a while. I had slippers for Christmas once. It was like putting your feet inside a lion's head. They had a mane made of strands of wool, the colour bracken goes in the autumn. Used to grow in the Cornish hedges. Don't know if it still does. Haven't been there for a while.

Anyway, those slippers made me think. They brought back that time I used to play with my mate Jamie. Till his mum wouldn't let him come round to my house any more.

I've spent the whole morning thinking about Christmas, and I don't want to move. Jamie knocked at our front door on Boxing Day. He was standing next to the best bike I've ever seen. Red frame, striped saddle, a huge bell, stabilisers.

'Coming out?' he asked.

'I'll ask my mum.'

She said yes of course. Didn't want me hanging about the house with my dad at home. So off I went. Wearing my new slippers. My head was concentrating on that shiny new bike you see, and how I might just get a go on it. I didn't notice I'd still got my lion slippers on my feet. Not until I the hit the puddle that is. I felt my stomach go to jelly. I started to cry. I was only five after all. Five-year-olds do cry, don't they?

'What's up?' yelled Jamie. He did a turn and came tearing back towards me.

'You can have a go in a minute.'

'It's me slippers,' I said.

We both looked at the lion faces. Wet, muddy, and sort of sorrowful.

'Your mum can wash them.' Jamie put his foot on the pedal again. 'Go and ask her.'

My dad was standing at the front door. Fingering his belt.

'Get in,' he said.

I'm not saying I had an unhappy childhood. I'll just say I knew the feel on a belt on my bare skin, the pain as my mum cleaned the blood off, the itch of the welts as they healed. The ache of bruised limbs. I knew that all right.

My mum rescued those slippers from the bin, washed the mud off, told me to keep them hidden from my dad.

I thought about being a pavement artist the other day. Old Charlie laughed. Said I'd be better joining him, asked if I wanted a sip. I said no thanks, my mum used meths to clean ink stains off my school shirt.

The worst kind of shoes are high heels. Sometimes when the street's not busy, I hear a clip-clopping and I know there's a pair on the way. I don't look higher than the ankles. Why would I want to see a face I'll never know, never speak to? Now I'll have to think about something else pretty quick, or I'll have to fight down the urge to cry. Big boys don't blub. My dad taught me that.

Plymouth's not a bad place to be when the sun shines. I like the way the kids chase the pigeons, the way those daft birds flitter away. I like the seagulls, how they stamp on the grass for worms. I do look up when nobody's about. I like the way the light changes the colour of the leaves, the way the clouds move across the sky.

It's when the people come that I look down. Watch the shoes. I know when to keep my mouth shut too.

Voices toss out words. Get a job. Get off your backside. Down and out.

The feet move on. Sometimes people stop, give me a bottle of water, a sandwich. Most nights I get a bed. Once or twice I've found the hostels full. Then it's a doorway here, a bench there. I know who to avoid. I haven't touched drugs since I left home.

I'm thinking of Cornwall again, the spiky yellow gorse and the rough pink heather, riding the cliffs, enduring the wind, the storms. Surviving.

I had an offer last night. Don't get me wrong. I was sleeping at the refuge, Sally Army, you know? There's a woman there, cheery, looks us in the eye. She said she might be able to help me. I'd be fixed up with clothes, somewhere to stay, till I got on my feet. She saw me hesitating. Her eyes lost their sparkle for a moment.

'Please,' she said. 'Think about it carefully.'

I'm not up to it. I've been on the road too long. Watching the feet has become my normal way of life.

A regular job? Nah. Couldn't even get there on time.

Besides, how do I know I won't turn out to be just like my dad?

Stuff the offer. I won't go back. She can find someone else. A pair of green high heels click towards me, disappear out of range. Crocs, sandals, flip-flops, brogues. The shoes of the city pass me by.

THE TIGHTROPE WALKER

On 23rd June 2013, Nik Wallenda crossed the Little Colorado River Gorge in the Grand Canyon on a high wire.

My life is more treacherous than his. Every day I walk my own tightrope.

Dan leaves the house early, by a quarter to eight at the latest, and I'm left giving the girls their breakfast, helping them find their PE kit, their library books, their tuck money. I've told them to pack their bags the night before.

'All set for tomorrow?' I ask.

'Yes, Mummy,' says Molly, and she usually is. Katya stares and stomps out of the room. At nine and three quarters, and ten and a half, they should be old enough to be responsible for some things in their lives. Surely.

And so I go on, footstep by footstep.

'Fiona.' That's what Dan's daughter calls me on a good day. 'Molly's hidden my homework.'

Molly freezes. Her lip trembles. 'No, I haven't.'

'Where is it then?' Katya narrows her eyes.

'I don't know.'

I can see where this is going. Molly's going to cry, I'll cuddle her, and Katya will accuse me of siding with her again.

I sigh. It's no use asking why the homework isn't in the bag already, but I do it anyway.

'Why are you always picking on me?' shouts Katya.

On the outside I am calm. 'Go and look for your book.'

'You're not my mother. You can't tell me what to do.'

'I am the adult in charge of you at the moment,' I reply firmly. 'So go and look for your book.'

'Right,' says Katya as she clumps away up the stairs, 'I'm telling Dad you wouldn't help me.'

Molly starts crying, and the whole morning charade is underway in only a slightly different form from yesterday.

On the way to school, I look in the mirror and see Katya's lower lip jutting forward, her face dark with anger, and I can hear Molly snivelling. At the gate I try to smile equally at both of them. I give Molly a hug. Katya pulls away from me, glowering.

'See you later, girls.' Tears prick my eyes.

Katya runs off and I see her bump into another child on purpose. Molly clings to my hand.

'I don't like Katya. I wish we didn't have to live with them.'

'You like Dan, don't you?'

Molly nods.

'It's early days, love.'

'It's been since January, Mummy. That's six months.' Molly's crying again. 'I don't like Katya. She's horrible.'

The whistle blows, and Molly lets go of me.

Every day my tightrope wobbles, and I daren't look beyond the next step.

When Nik Wallenda crossed the Little Colorado River Gorge, he had no safety harness. Nik's walk was on a two-inch-thick steel cable, 1,500 feet in the air. The quarter of a mile took him 22 minutes.

I have no idea how long my tightrope is, just that every step is treacherous. In my lunch break I sit in the café with a jacket potato, and try to see a way to improve the lives of the two people I love most in the world, Dan and Molly, and one feisty ten-year-old I planned to win round with kindness and love. I'd thought it would be easy. How foolish I'd been.

I chew coleslaw absent-mindedly. Dan is a kind and lovely person. He says the divorce was messy; he says Katya's mother has moved to a new life three hundred miles away. She didn't want to take Katya with her.

I'd met Dan's daughter lots of times of course, mostly when Molly was off with her dad for the weekend. Katya's the sort of girl who'd rather be climbing a tree or bouncing on a trampoline, than playing Scrabble or Othello, things Molly likes to do. She was always very polite when Dan and I took her out. It was only when we told her about our plan to live together that she started to change. Or perhaps she was like it anyway, and I simply couldn't see beyond the face of the man I love.

'She's becoming a teenager a bit early,' Dan said. 'She's a good kid.'

As far as I can tell, she isn't anything like a good kid. As Molly said this morning, she's horrible.

I look around the café guiltily. I am appalled that I've had that thought. What makes it worse is that whenever I try and talk to Dan about Katya, he sides with her, he really does. And I suppose I always side with Molly.

I start the afternoon with only half my mind on my job, recording the state of people's teeth, suctioning a patient's mouth, passing the dentist sterile tools. It doesn't seem fair: Dan and I have a chance of happiness together, and that child is doing everything she can to spoil it.

'She'll get used to you,' Dan says.

Once, when things were really bad for me and Molly, he looked sadly at me.

'This isn't working, is it?'

And then he said he was sorry, it was probably his fault. He has so much marking to do, so much lesson preparation, perhaps he hasn't been fair in asking me to come and share his life.

I think about the tightrope walker, Nik Wallenda. He came from a long line of circus performers. Tightrope walking was in his genes. His mother made him a pair of elk-skin soled shoes to keep a grip on the cable as he took step after step. And not only that, he was murmuring prayers almost constantly along the way.

I haven't prayed for a long time. I don't think I believe in prayer any more. I look out of the window, in between patients, speak silently to a god I don't believe in. Nothing remarkable happens. A bus goes past in the street below, the hygienist pops in to speak to the dentist.

I've started to dread going home in the evening. Perhaps I was expecting too much. Maybe I should listen to Molly, pack our bags and leave. Step off the tightrope, move back into our life before Dan.

I pick up the girls from their after school club. Katya's sitting on a chair holding her arm. She looks paler than usual.

'Are you OK, love?'

She starts crying.

'Hey, what is it? Do you feel poorly.'

'She had a fight with someone at break,' says the carer. 'She's in big trouble. There's a letter for her father in her bag.'

'I've been suspended.' She speaks without emotion.

The tightrope seems to sway beneath my feet.

'I'd better get you home.' What else can I say?

In the car, Molly breaks the silence. She's keen to tell me about the story she's written. Her teacher says it's her best one ever.

'Creep,' says Katya, and Molly stops.

'I'll tell you later, Mummy,' she whispers, and I know she's almost crying again.

Katya's still clutching her arm as we walk into the house.

'You'd better let me have a look at that.' I say.

'I'm showing Dad,' she says.

I pour glasses of squash for the girls. I suggest Molly might like to watch a video, while I talk to Katya.

'Well done about the story,' I say. 'I'm very proud of you.'

'Nobody's proud of me,' says Katya.

'I think we should talk. Off you go Molly.'

'I want Dad,' says Katya.

'Look love, your dad's not going to be home for a while, so why don't you try talking to me. Maybe I can help.'

'You can't. Besides, you're not my mother.'

'I wish I was,' I say, 'then you'd let me help, wouldn't you?'

She stares at me. She hasn't seen her mother since she left the city. No wonder the poor kid's angry. Every day she sees me with Molly, the two of us talking like friends. We are friends. Every other weekend she watches as Molly goes off with her father, a man she trusts, a man who loves her.

Like me, Katya's on a tightrope. One parent's gone. Who's to say the other won't get fed up with her, push her out of his life. Though I know Dan won't do that, and surely Katya must know too.

Katya picks up her drink and I follow her up the stairs with my mug of tea. There's a small sofa in her room, where her friends can sit. Only they haven't been for a while. Maybe they're fed up with someone who pushes people for nothing, someone who picks fights, someone who is angry all the time.

'I don't want you in my room,' she says.

'I want to help.'

'You can't.' Katya bangs her door in my face.

Downstairs I chop vegetables viciously, stir onions forcefully round the pan. What right had I to bring my daughter into this house, into this atmosphere which is destroying us? My tightrope wobbles dangerously. I haven't got Nik Wallenda's strength of character. I've had enough. I want to pack my bag, take Molly's hand, and go.

Dan comes home, comments on the delicious smell, sees my face, holds me.

I tell him about Katya, that she's in trouble at school, that I wanted to help, and she wouldn't talk to me.

Dan goes upstairs, knocks at Katya's door. He's with her for a long time. Molly asks me if it's nearly dinner time, and I hug her and say,' Not quite.' We both hear Dan come out of Katya's bedroom. I'll tell him this evening, that I think it'd be better if Molly and I leave.

I hear Katya shouting from the top of the stairs.

'No I will not. She's not my mother.'

I stand by the kitchen door, holding on to Molly's shoulder. Dan's footsteps stop. His voice is quiet, controlled.

'No, thank God,' he says.

I think of Nik Wallenda, whose mother made him that pair of elk-skin shoes to keep a grip on the cable as he moved. He would have fallen off but for her thoughtfulness, her faith in him, her courage.

'Your mother abandoned you, Kat. She doesn't want to see you ever again. Fiona is prepared to love you, if you will only give her a chance.'

'You're hurting me, Mummy.'

I let go of Molly's shoulder.

Dan thumps the banister. 'And if you start being nice to Molly, she might let you be her sister.'

He comes downstairs, white-faced.

Katya's very quiet during dinner. She keeps looking at her father, but he can't or won't meet her eyes. She seems small, broken almost, a child who doesn't know how to make her pain go away. She'll be better off by far if Molly and I disappear out of her life.

At bedtime, I sit on Molly's bed and we talk. It's like old times. I go into the room I share with Dan, lift my suitcase from the top of the wardrobe, begin to pack some of my clothes.

'What are you doing?' Dan's running his hand through his hair.

'It's no good, Dan. She'll never accept me, and her behaviour's getting worse.'

He stares at me for a moment. I want him to argue, to try and persuade me to stay, but he doesn't.

He knows it's for the best then.

My tightrope's wobbling badly now. I wish I had the equivalent of those elk-skin shoes. I wish I was somebody else, anyone except me.

I fill my case, close the lid, pull the zip slowly round it.

There's a tug at my sleeve. I turn, expecting Molly. It's Katya. She looks very young in her pink nightie. She's holding a teddy bear. Her face is blotchy, her eyes red.

She hesitates, throws herself into my arms, weeping. We are both weeping.

'Don't go, Fiona.'

The wire still wobbles as Nik Wallenda steps towards dry land.

AUTHOR'S COMMENTS: CLOUD PAINTINGS
~ Facing life's challenges ~

The characters in these stories are all battling against something. They want to survive, to beat the challenges life has thrown at them. Creating a story can sometimes be an opportunity to get to know and understand other people, to see the world through their eyes. My characters are all fictitious, but I hope they resemble real people you might know, or someone you might pass in a busy street.

INTO THE RAIN won 1st prize in the 2012 Tenby Arts Festival competition. I was inspired to write it after a friend told me how, on visiting days, she used to help run a crèche at her local prison. *Into The Rain* has not been published before.

THE GARDENER won 2nd prize in the 2014 Writers' News competition for a story about an oddball. It was published online at https://www.writers-online.co.uk/writing-competitions/showcase

CLOUD PAINTINGS won 3rd prize in the 2013 Ilkley Literature Festival competition. During the years I taught four- to six-year-olds, several of the children lost a parent, due to illness or sudden death. It's a huge thing for any family to cope with. I felt moved to write Cloud Paintings after all the children I knew had grown up. My characters are fictitious, but I hope the story holds a deep truth about the difficulties of a family's bereavement. *Cloud Paintings* has not been published before.

A PERFECT WORLD won 1st prize in the 2012 Greenacre Writers competition. I wanted to explore what it is like to be the child of a mother who didn't want children, and who could never quite come to terms with her unexpected son. *A Perfect World* was published in the *Greenacre Writers Anthology Volume 2* and at http://greenacrewriters.blogspot.co.uk/

A HOLE IN THE SKY won 2nd prize in the 2013 Ifanca Hélène James short story competition. A young man is confined to a wheelchair after an accident, and the last thing he wants is for people to feel sorry for him. He is angry. How will he ever move on? *A Hole in the Sky* was published on the website at https://ifancahelenejames.wordpress.com/to-apply/

SHOES won 1st prize in the 2011 Mags4dorset competition. It was inspired by a homeless man called Andy, who was always grateful for a mug of coffee or a sandwich. He used to sell *The Big Issue* outside WH Smith's in Plymouth, and one day he was no longer there. Did he find a job, and a new way of life? I shall probably never know. *Shoes* was published in the December 2011 issue of *Town and Village Magazine*.

THE TIGHTROPE WALKER was a runner-up in the 2013 Greenacre Writers short story competition. I wanted to consider how difficult life is for a step-parent to an angry child. *The Tightrope Walker* was published in the *Greenacre Writers Anthology Volume 3*.

ABOUT THE AUTHOR

Veronica Bright is a prize-winning author of short fiction and drama. In 2005 she won the *Woman and Home* Short Story Competition with *Out of the Apple Tree*, which was subsequently published in *The Sunday Night Book Club* anthology (Arrow Books). Since then her work has won prizes in almost forty competitions.

Veronica and her family came to live in Cornwall in 1988, and she has since claimed to be Cornish by adoption. For many years she taught the youngest children in a village primary school. She misses her own children now they've grown up and left home, but appreciates having time to write. Interruptions are always welcome if accompanied by tea and chocolate biscuits.

Veronica is represented by Kiran Kataria of the Keane Kataria Literary Agency. She writes a monthly blog on her website: www.veronicabright.co.uk

Printed in Great Britain
by Amazon